This
PJ BOOK
belongs to

PJ Library®

JEWISH BEDTIME STORIES and SONGS

This one is for Hannah —P.M.

For Poulbot, the king of lignerolles —C.D.

PJ Library, a program of the Harold Grinspoon Foundation
67 Hunt Street, Suite 100
Agawam, MA 01001
U.S.A.

Designed by Michael Grinley

First Edition
10 9 8 7 6 5 4 3 2 1
091926.4K1/B1448/A6
Printed in China

The Mouse
Who Danced the Hora

Written by Pamela Mayer • Illustrated by Christine Davenier

In a teeny tiny hole in the wall of the social hall at Temple Sholom
there lives a little mouse.

Her name is Tillie Mouscovitz.

When Tillie hears music she peeks out the door of her mouse house. Music means a celebration at Temple Sholom's social hall.

"A wedding reception, how nice!" Tillie says. "May the bride and groom know nothing but happiness."

Tillie's whiskers twitch as the band plays her favorite song.

"Such nice music! Now everyone will dance the hora."

If only Tillie could join the circle and dance the hora too, just as the people do at many Temple Sholom celebrations!

"But for a mouse, it's not," Tillie says.

Stepping forward with the left foot towards the right and then forward with the right foot to match, the people turn this way and that as they dance in a large circle.

Tillie dances too, singing in her wee mouse voice, "*Hava nagila, hava nagila, hava nagila, v'nismecha.*"

The dancers stand in place and clap their hands. Tillie scurries forward and claps her paws together too.

Two chairs are carried into the center of the circle, one for the bride, one for the groom. The chairs are lifted up high.

Tillie giggles. "It is a *mitzvah*, a good deed, to make the bride and groom happy on their wedding day."

The bride and groom sway in their chairs. The people dance around them. The band plays, and Tillie scampers right into the hora circle.

The bride and groom, still seated in their chairs, are brought
back down to the floor. Everyone else runs away.
 Tillie looks at the bride and groom.
 The bride and groom look back at Tillie.

Stepping forward with her left paw, Tillie brings her right paw to match. She steps behind with her left paw and again brings the right to match. Tillie turns this way and that.

"This little mouse is dancing the hora," the groom says.
The bride smiles. "She is."

Standing as one, the bride and groom push away their chairs. They form a circle around Tillie and dance. Tillie dances too.

The musicians play the hora song once more: "*Hava nagila, hava nagila, hava nagila*…let us rejoice, let us rejoice, let us rejoice…"

One by one, then two by two, the wedding guests return to the
dance floor.
"…*v'nemischa*…and be glad…"

When the song ends, Tillie bows low. She hears a cheer and then another as everyone claps for her.

Tillie's whiskers twitch with happiness. "So much joy! Such celebration! How nice it is to dance the hora!"

The tired little mouse hurries home. She is asleep as soon as her head touches the pillow.

Tillie wakes in the middle of the night. She yawns and stretches. Temple Sholom is dark and quiet. The wedding ended long ago.

Tillie's tummy growls. "So maybe I'll find a crumb of challah, a morsel of cheese left over."

Right outside her door is a surprise, a teeny tiny slice of wedding cake just the right size. Next to it is a note which reads,